TORNADOES

SEYMOUR SIMON

Updated Edition

HARPER

An Imprint of HarperCollinsPublishers

To Liz Nealon, my wife and helpmate

Special thanks to Erik Rasmussen

PHOTO AND ART CREDITS: Page 2: © Jim Reed/Science Source; page 4: © Warren Faidley/Corbis; page 7: © Jason Persoff Stormdoctor/Science Source; pages 10–11: © Jim Reed/Science Source; page 13: © Bettmann/Corbis; page 15: Courtesy NOAA News; page 17: Hulton Archive/Getty; page 19: © Jim Edds/Science Source; page 21: © Eric Nguyen/Corbis; page 23: © Simon Brewer/Corbis; pages 24–25: © Jim Reed/Science Source; pages 26–27: © Jim Reed/Science Source; page 28: © Jim Reed/Corbis; pages 30–31:© Visuals Unlimited/Corbis
Art on page 9 by Ann Neumann

ISBN 978-0-06-247033-1 (trade bdg.) — ISBN 978-0-06-247032-4 (pbk.)

16 17 18 19 20 SCP 10 9 8 7 6 5 4 3 2 1

❖

Revised edition, 2017

Author's Note

From a young age, I was interested in animals, space, my surroundings—all the natural sciences. When I was a teenager, I became the president of a nationwide junior astronomy club with a thousand members. After college, I became a classroom teacher for nearly twenty-five years while also writing articles and books for children on science and nature even before I became a full-time writer. My experience as a teacher gives me the ability to understand how to reach my young readers and get them interested in the world around us.

I've written more than 300 books, and I've thought a lot about different ways to encourage interest in the natural world, as well as how to show the joys of nonfiction. When I write, I use comparisons to help explain unfamiliar ideas, complex concepts, and impossibly large numbers. I try to engage your senses and imagination to set the scene and to make science fun. For example, in *Penguins*, I emphasize the playful nature of these creatures on the very first page by mentioning how penguins excel at swimming and diving. I use strong verbs to enhance understanding. I make use of descriptive detail and ask questions that anticipate what you may be thinking (sometimes right at the start of the book).

Many of my books are photo-essays, which use extraordinary photographs to amplify and expand the text, creating different and engaging ways of exploring nonfiction. You'll also find a glossary, an index, and website and research recommendations in most of my books, which make them ideal for enhancing your reading and learning experience. As William Blake wrote in his poem, I want my readers "to see a world in a grain of sand, / And a heaven in a wild flower, / Hold infinity in the palm of your hand, / And eternity in an hour."

Seymour Simon

Twisters, whirlwinds, waterspouts, cyclones—tornadoes go by different names. But whatever they are called, the roaring winds of a tornado can toss a truck high into the air, smash a building, and snap the trunk of a tree like a matchstick.

A tornado's **funnel** sometimes looks like a huge elephant's trunk hanging down from a cloud. The funnel acts like a giant vacuum cleaner—whenever the hose touches the ground, it sucks things up into the air.

Tornadoes (from the Spanish word *tronada*, meaning "**thunderstorm**") have been reported in every state of the United States and in every season. However, they occur most often in the eastern two-thirds of the country during the spring, which is sometimes called tornado season.

A tornado is a powerfully twisting column of air that makes contact with the ground. It is visible when it contains water droplets in the form of a cloud, or surface dust and **debris**, or some of both. When a tornado touches down, it usually leaves a cloud of dust and wreckage on the ground. If the twisting column of air is not very strong, it doesn't pull in debris and is not visible. When the whirling air becomes strong enough to pull in dust and debris, it makes the twister visible as a tornado.

All tornadoes are local storms. A typical tornado is four hundred to five hundred feet wide, yet still extends tens of thousands of feet from cloud to ground, and has winds of less than 112 miles per hour. It usually lasts only a few minutes and covers only a few miles on the ground. But a few monster tornadoes are a mile wide, can reach upward of thirty thousand feet, and have the strongest winds ever measured in nature: up to three hundred miles per hour. They can last for an hour or more and travel more than two hundred miles along the ground, leaving enormous damage in their wake.

The first step in the birth of a tornado is usually a thunderstorm. Heavy rain produces a downdraft, which makes the air along the ground move in a kind of rolling pin action. The spinning air pushes underneath an updraft, where warm humid air rises from the ground. As these updrafts cool in the upper atmosphere, the moisture in them forms clouds. The water droplets or ice crystals in the clouds grow bigger as water vapor around them condenses, or becomes liquid. The droplets or crystals begin to fall, creating downdrafts, and these downdrafts meet new spinning updrafts, which continue feeding warm humid air into the spreading thunderhead cloud. This is the most violent time in a thunderstorm, as the air begins to spin faster and faster.

Weather in North America is often caused by **air masses** and **fronts**. Air masses can be cool or warm, moist or dry. For example, cool dry air comes from northern lands, while warm moist air comes from the Gulf of Mexico and the Pacific Ocean. Air masses push each other across the lines where they meet, which are called fronts.

Large-scale weather systems that contain air masses, fronts, and upper atmosphere winds called **jet streams** sometimes combine to form and grow large storms and tornadoes. The keys to tornado formation are to have warm moist air near the ground and cool air above. This gives the storms energy as the warm air rises rapidly. Another key is to have strong upper winds blowing at an angle to lower winds. This gives the storm a spinning top. The third key is to have the storms kicked into motion by the rapid movements of air masses along the ground.

Sometimes a rapidly spinning thunderstorm, called a **supercell**, forms from a smaller storm. Supercells often develop spinning winds inside them called **mesocyclones**. Some die out after a few minutes, while others spin faster and form funnel clouds at their bases. The strongest tornadoes form in association with mesocyclones.

Supercells are most common between April and June, and they are most likely to occur in an area known as tornado alley, which runs from central Texas as far north as Illinois and Indiana and as far east as Kentucky. From November to April, supercells form in some southern states, and from July through September, they can occur in the Southwest and the Northeast.

Tornadoes born in supercells are hugely powerful. One monster tornado that touched down in Illinois in 1990 lifted a twenty-ton trailer truck from a highway and bounced it up and down like a ball before depositing it in a field eleven hundred feet away. A strong tornado can completely destroy a building and leave just a mass of wreckage behind.

Sometimes tornadoes do odd things. A tornado once sucked up a pond full of frogs and rained them down on a nearby town. Another tornado struck a house and carried a five-hundred-pound piano twelve hundred feet through the air. The worst tornado in recent years hit the town of Joplin, Missouri, on May 22, 2011.

In 2011, a tornado struck Joplin, Missouri, at dinnertime and was on the ground for thirty-two minutes. The path of the tornado stretched a mile wide and the storm gained strength as it moved through Joplin.

The town's hospital took a direct hit from the tornado. Every window in the building blew out, the top two floors were ripped off, and patients in the emergency room were sucked out through the broken windows and into the parking lot.

By the time the tornado left, 161 people were killed, more than 1,000 were injured, and 2.8 billion dollars in damage had been done. The Joplin tornado was the deadliest in the United States since 1947.

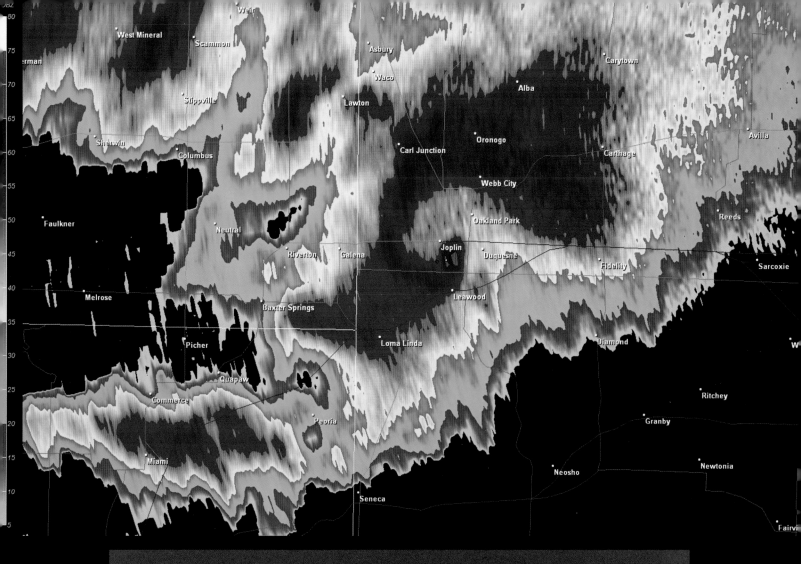

This is a radar image depicting the supercell thunderstorm that produced the monster EF-5 multiple-vortex tornado that hit Joplin, Missouri, on May 22, 2011. The colors show the intensity of rain, hail, and debris being kicked up by the storm.

The single deadliest tornado in history was the Tri-State tornado. It touched down in Missouri on March 18, 1925, and then swept into Illinois and then Indiana, traveling along a 219-mile path of death and destruction. In three and a half hours, the tornado killed 689 people, injured 2,000, and left more than 10,000 homeless. As F. S. Short, a witness to the disaster, described to the *Daily Independent* on April 16, 1925, "One great swipe and it brushed through the city in less than a moment's time. . . ."

Most tornadoes come singly, but a number of storms produce multiple tornadoes on the same day. On April 27, 2011, a series of destructive tornadoes, known as the 2011 Super Tornado Outbreak, hit the southeastern United States. The one-day weather event was among the deadliest on record, with 199 tornadoes barreling across fifteen states at speeds of 45 to 70 miles per hour. By the time it was over, 316 people had died and more than 2,400 had been injured. The gang of tornadoes destroyed hundreds of homes, schools, and other buildings, and some people were sucked out of their homes. As James Sykes, a resident of Tuscaloosa, Alabama, noted in a *CNN* article on April 28, 2011, it was "like a silent monster . . . moving at a steady rate and demolishing everything in its path."

Fortunately, not all tornadoes are as violent and destructive as the Tri-State tornado of 1925 or the April 2011 tornadoes. Most tornadoes are much weaker.

Murphysboro, Illinois, after Tri-State tornado of 1925

It's nearly impossible to measure wind speeds inside tornadoes because they destroy weather instruments in their paths. That's why a measurement system was devised to measure a storm's strength by its impact on ground structures and vegetation. The original Fujita Scale (named after Ted Fujita, a storm research scientist) came out in 1971. At that time, there was only limited information to base the wind speed ranges for each intensity. Since then, weather scientists have much more information to draw upon, so they have refined the wind speed numbers and the scale is now called the **Enhanced Fujita Scale**, or EF-Scale.

EF-0 tornadoes have winds that range from 65 to 80 miles per hour. They cause minor damage to houses: blowing off shingles, peeling back sections of roofs, or damaging gutters or sidings. They break off branches of trees and may uproot smaller, shallow-rooted trees. Nearly three out of every ten tornadoes are classed as EF-0.

Slightly greater damage is caused by EF-1 tornadoes. These blow at 86 to 110 miles per hour. They cause moderate damage to homes, break windows and exterior doors, and damage roofs and shingles. They may overturn or badly damage mobile homes. They push cars and trailers around on the ground and uproot some medium-sized trees. About four out of every ten tornadoes are in the EF-1 class.

Strong tornadoes are classed as EF-2 and EF-3. EF-2 tornadoes have winds of between 111 and 135 miles per hour. They cause considerable damage. EF-2 tornadoes may blow roofs off well-constructed homes, leaving only strong walls standing. They demolish sheds and small outbuildings. They can also overturn mobile homes, cause walls of wooden buildings to collapse, and lift cars off the ground. About two to three of every ten tornadoes are classed as EF-2.

EF-3 tornadoes cause severe damage, since they have winds ranging from 136 to 165 miles per hour. These tornadoes can flatten all the trees in a forest and collapse metal buildings. They blow off roofs and tumble exterior walls made of concrete blocks. Six out of every hundred tornadoes are classed as EF-3.

The most violent tornadoes are classed as EF-4 or EF-5. An EF-4 tornado has wind speeds of 166 to 200 miles per hour. Such powerful winds cause extreme damage. The winds will leave few if any walls standing, even in sturdily built apartment houses. EF-4 tornadoes can pluck trees up from their roots and break their trunks in half. They can pick up and throw large building materials long distances, hurling them with such force that the materials penetrate concrete. Only two out of every hundred tornadoes are classed as EF-4.

EF-5 tornadoes—the highest classification on the EF-Scale—are the monster tornadoes. Their winds blow at speeds of more than two hundred miles per hour. They can cause incredible damage, including leveling almost any small- or medium-sized building and making the land look as if a bulldozer roared across it. EF-5 tornadoes are the rarest. Fewer than one out of every hundred tornadoes is classed as EF-5.

Learning about tornadoes can save lives. For example, even though the average tornado travels at thirty miles per hour, much faster ground speeds—up to seventy miles per hour—have been reported. That means that trying to flee to safety in an automobile may be reasonable in the country, where the roads are not crowded. But in populated areas, traffic-clogged roads can make it dangerous to get into an automobile.

It is also untrue that tornadoes never strike big cities. For example, Atlanta, Georgia, was struck by a tornado on March 14, 2008. It hit the Philips Arena, where an NBA game was under way. Many buildings were damaged and two large hotels had to be evacuated when the windows blew out. And in the past forty years, storm-prone St. Louis, Missouri, has been hit by tornadoes more than forty-five times.

Still another myth is that opening the windows in a house will help prevent it from being destroyed by a tornado. In fact, opening the wrong windows could allow air to rush in and blow the structure apart from inside. The best advice is to forget the windows and get to a shelter.

One of the most important things you can do to prevent injury in a tornado is to be alert to the onset of severe weather. Learn the signs of approaching bad weather so that you will know to tune in to the weather forecasts on television or the radio. If a tornado watch is issued for your area, it means a tornado is possible. If a tornado warning is issued, it means a tornado has been spotted either on the ground or on radar.

Here are some of the things people hear or see just before a tornado arrives:

- There is a sound a little like rushing air or a waterfall, and it turns into a roar as the tornado comes closer.

- Debris drops from the sky.

- A rotating cloud extends downward toward or close to the ground. It is spinning, while other clouds are moving very quickly toward it.

If a tornado watch or warning is posted, then a real danger sign that a tornado is coming is falling **hail**. This is especially true for the Great Plains in the United States.

It is also a good idea to know, *before* a tornado strikes, where to go for shelter. Cars, trailers, and mobile homes are *not* safe during a tornado. Go to the basement of a solidly built house or any sturdy structure. Staying under the stairs or a heavy table helps to protect you from crumbling walls. Blankets can also help to shield you from flying debris. Putting on a helmet may also help protect you.

In an apartment or a home without a basement, an inside room or closet is the safest place. Getting into a bathtub and putting a couch cushion over you helps protect you on all sides. Bathtubs are usually solidly anchored to the ground and sometimes are the only things left in place after a tornado hits.

If you are out walking or biking and are caught in the open when a tornado touches down, lie flat in a ditch or low area if there is *no* rain. If there *is* rain, there may be a danger of flash flooding. Then you should take shelter away from trees and power lines and away from glass windows or doors in houses. Crouch down and make yourself as small a target as possible.

Weather scientists, called meteorologists, are trying to find the best ways to predict and warn against tornadoes. One thing they do is to keep a close watch on severe thunderstorms. In the Great Plains of the United States, **weather spotters** may also look for rapidly rotating clouds, which can spawn a tornado. The National Weather Service uses **Doppler radar**, which can show air movement as well as the shape of the **precipitation** area. Early signs of rapid air rotation during a thunderstorm can allow life-saving warnings to be issued fifteen to twenty minutes before a tornado forms.

Each year about a thousand tornadoes touch down in the United States, far more than in any other country in the world. Only a small number actually strike occupied buildings, but every year hundreds of people are killed or injured. Still, the chances that a tornado will strike you or a building that you are in are very, very small. In fact, you are about as likely to be hit by lightning or to be the victim of a shark attack as to be struck by a tornado.

The best protection from tornadoes comes from receiving an early warning. Listening to local radio or television stations during a weather watch can alert you to take safety measures as soon as a tornado warning is broadcast. You don't have to worry too much in advance about tornadoes, but finding out when they are coming and knowing what to do is certain to help you if one strikes.

GLOSSARY

Air mass—A body of air extending hundreds or thousands of miles horizontally and sometimes as high as the stratosphere.

Debris—The pieces that are left after something has been destroyed.

Doppler radar—A radar tracking system that uses the Doppler effect to determine the location and velocity of storms, clouds, precipitation, and other weather phenomena.

Enhanced Fujita Scale—Updated version of Fujita Scale created in 2006. It is still a damage-based scale but more closely examines wind speeds in relation to storm damage.

Front—A boundary between two air masses of different properties such as temperature and humidity.

Funnel—A hollow cone with a smaller end that tapers off.

Hail—Precipitation in the form of small balls or lumps usually made up of clear ice and compact snow.

Jet stream—A strong current of fast winds high above the earth's surface; also known as upper atmosphere winds.

Mesocyclone—A rapidly rotating air mass within a thunderstorm that often gives rise to a tornado.

Precipitation—Rain, snow, sleet, or hail that falls to the ground.

Supercell—An unusually large air mass that contains updrafts and downdrafts in convective loops and moves and reacts as a single unit.

Thunderstorm—A storm with lightning and thunder.

Weather spotter—A person who helps identify and describe severe local storms. He or she gives real-time reports of hail size, wind damage, flash flooding, heavy rain, tornadoes, and waterspouts to effectively warn the public of the dangerous weather condition.

INDEX
Bold type indicates illustrations.

READ MORE ABOUT IT

Seymour Simon's website
www.seymoursimon.com

climatekids.nasa.gov/menu/
weather-and-climate

www.education.noaa.gov/
Weather_and_Atmosphere/
Tornadoes.html

www.weather.gov/cae/
justforkids.html